JOSEPH KUEFLER

BEYOND
the
POND

Balzer + Bray
An Imprint of HarperCollinsPublishers

To Andrew —
This is one of our favorite books
and we hope you enjoy it too. Wishing
you a very Happy Birthday and lots
of adventures in the coming year!
Your friends
Henry & Vivienne
March 2019

To Jonah, for showing me
what lies beyond everything

Balzer + Bray
is an imprint of HarperCollins Publishers.

Beyond the Pond

ISBN 978-0-06-236427-2

The artist used a combination of mixed media and photographed textures, as well as Adobe
Photoshop and Illustrator, to create the digital illustrations for this book.
Typography by Martha Rago. Hand lettering by Joseph Kuefler
17 18 19   SCP   10 9 8 7 6 5 4
❖
First Edition

Just behind an ordinary house filled with too little fun, Ernest D. had decided today would be the day that he'd explore the depths of his pond.

So he tried
sticking a stick . . .

and dipping a hook . . .

and sinking a stone,
but nothing touched.

"My pond has no
bottom," said Ernest D.

"My pond goes on forever! I've always
wanted to explore a pond with no bottom!

"Oh, how exceptional!"

So Ernest D. gathered his explorer supplies . . .

stretched three times,
and prepared to set off.

"I hope they allow dogs
down there," he said.

And with that,
Ernest D. dove . . .

down between the fishes and the frogs,
past the squid and sharks and shapeless
things, into his pond forever deep.

He dove into lightless stretches
and through sunken treasures.

"I think someone forgot to turn on the lights in this part of my pond," he said.

Ernest D. dove farther into his pond
than anyone had ever gone before . . .

until, at last, he came up on the other side.

The other side of his
pond was big.

And raucous.

It was oh so tiny,

oh so tall,

and every shape in between.

Best of all, it was just for him.

But this new place was
other things too. . . .

It was ghoulish

and ghastly.

It was all things unimaginable.

But Ernest D. was the
bravest of explorers.

He battled and brawled
until the moon ducked low.

And in the moment between moonset
and sunrise, Ernest D. looked upon the
endlessness of his newly discovered land.

"All this was hiding in a pond,"
said Ernest D. "How exceptional."

So he returned to his pond, stretched three times . . .

and dove . . .

back into lightless caverns and through
sunken treasures, past the squid and sharks
and shapeless things, out of his pond and
back into the world.

But the world wasn't quite as he'd left it.
His house seemed a little less small.

And his town looked a little less ordinary . . . .
Beyond every street and silent corner was a
place unexplored.

"Exceptional," said Ernest D.